Making a Meal for a
MERMAID

by Ruth Owen

BEARPORT
PUBLISHING

Minneapolis, Minnesota

CREATE!

Credits:
Cover, © Shutterstock; 1, © Shafran/Shutterstock and © Ruby Tuesday Books; 3, © Shafran/
Shutterstock and © Shutterstock; 4T, © Shafran/Shutterstock and © Shutterstock; 5, © Shutterstock;
6, © Shafran/Shutterstock and © Ruby Tuesday Books; 7, © Ruby Tuesday Books and © Shutterstock;
8–9, © Ruby Tuesday Books and © Shutterstock; 10T, © Yellow Cat/Shutterstock; 10B, © Ruby Tuesday
Books; 11, © Ruby Tuesday Books and © Shutterstock; 12–13, © Ruby Tuesday Books; 14, © Ruby
Tuesday Books and © Shutterstock; 15, © Ruby Tuesday Books; 16, © Ruby Tuesday Books and
© Shutterstock; 17, © Ruby Tuesday Books and © Shutterstock; 18, © Gluiki/Shutterstock and © Ruby
Tuesday Books; 19, © Ruby Tuesday Books and © Shutterstock; 20, © Ruby Tuesday Books and
© Shutterstock; 21, © Ruby Tuesday Books; 22T, © Gehrke/Shutterstock; 22B, © Vkilikov/Shutterstock;
23TL, © Mangostar/Shutterstock; 23BL, © Shafran/Shutterstock; 23TR, © Africa Studio/Shutterstock;
23BR, © wavebreakmedia/Shutterstock.

President: Jen Jenson
Director of Product Development: Spencer Brinker
Senior Editor: Allison Juda
Associate Editor: Charly Haley
Designer: Colin O'Dea

Library of Congress Cataloging-in-Publication Data

Names: Owen, Ruth, 1967- author.
Title: Making a meal for a mermaid / by Ruth Owen.
Description: Minneapolis, Minnesota : Bearport Publishing Company, [2022] |
    Series: Mythical meals | "Create! books." | Includes bibliographical
    references and index.
Identifiers: LCCN 2020051874 (print) | LCCN 2020051875 (ebook) | ISBN
    9781636910659 (library binding) | ISBN 9781636910727 (ebook)
Subjects: LCSH: Cooking (Shrimp)–Juvenile literature. | Cooking
    (Pasta)–Juvenile literature. | LCGFT: Cookbooks.
Classification: LCC TX754.S58 O9 2022 (print) | LCC TX754.S58 (ebook) |
    DDC 641.6/95–dc23
LC record available at https://lccn.loc.gov/2020051874
LC ebook record available at https://lccn.loc.gov/2020051875

For more information, write to Bearport Publishing, 5357 Penn Avenue South,
Minneapolis, MN 55419. Printed in the United States of America.

Contents

A Marvelous Mermaid Meal.............. 4

DRINK
Lemon Ocean-ade 6

APPETIZER
Cheesy Pearl Seashells.............. 10

MAIN COURSE
Seaweed Pasta with Shrimp........ 14

DESSERT
Magical Mermaid Ice Cream....... 18

Mermaid Tales 22
Glossary.. 23
Index.. 24
Read More 24
Learn More Online................................. 24
About the Author.................................. 24

A Marvelous Mermaid Meal

A mermaid is coming for dinner! Get ready to impress your guest with a delicious **menu** that will remind her of her home under the waves.

◀ DRINK
Greet your mermaid friend with a glass of lemon ocean-ade that bubbles like waves crashing on a beach.

APPETIZER ▶
Your new friend snacks on **shellfish** in the sea. But she probably hasn't tasted anything as good as these crunchy, cheesy seashell **appetizers**.

◀ MAIN COURSE
For the main course, serve your guest shrimp and seaweed. But here's a little secret . . . the seaweed is made of pasta!

DESSERT ▶
Wow your guest with a bowl of creamy homemade ice cream for dessert. This treat is swirled with the colors of a mermaid's underwater world.

Get Ready to Cook!

- Always wash your hands with soap and hot water before you start cooking.

- Make sure your work surface and your cooking **equipment** are clean.

- Carefully read the recipe before you begin. If there's a step you don't understand, ask an adult for help.

- Gather all your supplies before you start.

- Carefully measure your **ingredients**. Your cooking will go better if you use the right amounts.

- When you've finished cooking, clean up the kitchen. Wash, dry, and put away your equipment.

Be Safe!

For some recipes, you'll need an adult helper. Be sure to ask for help when you use:

- Sharp objects, such as knives or scissors
- The oven, stove, or microwave
- An electric hand mixer

★ ☆ ★ ☆ ★   DRINK   ★ ☆ ★ ☆ ★

Lemon Ocean-ade

As a good **host**, you'll want to offer your guest a drink. Get the party started with glasses of delicious lemonade that will change into ocean colors as the ice cubes melt!

Makes 4 servings

Ingredients

- 6 cups water plus extra for making ice cubes
- Green, purple, and teal food coloring
- ¾ cup plus 4 tablespoons granulated sugar
- 4 lemons
- 2 teaspoons baking soda

Equipment

- 2 ice cube trays
- 3 toothpicks
- 3 small bowls
- 3 teaspoons
- A dinner plate
- A knife
- A lemon juicer
- A shallow dish
- 4 glasses
- A large pitcher
- A long-handled spoon

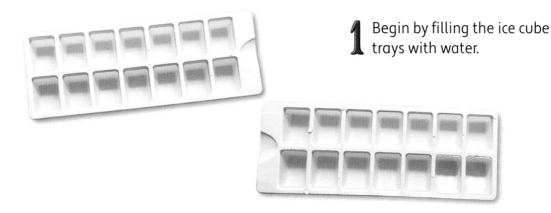

1 Begin by filling the ice cube trays with water.

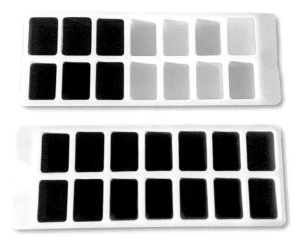

2 Put a drop of green, purple, or teal food coloring into each of the ice cube tray sections. Gently stir each section with a toothpick. Be sure to use a different toothpick for each color.

3 Carefully put the ice cube trays into the freezer.

4 To make colored sugar for decorating the glasses, evenly divide the ¾ cup of granulated sugar between the three small bowls.

5 Put 3 drops of green food coloring into one bowl and stir it into the sugar with a teaspoon. Keep stirring until all the sugar has turned green.

6 Repeat step 5 with the purple and teal food colorings and the two other bowls of sugar.

7 Carefully dump the sugar from each bowl onto a dinner plate, keeping the three colors separate. Spread the sugar out a little with a teaspoon, and then allow it to dry for about an hour. When the sugar is dry, mix the three colors together.

8 Ask an adult helper to cut the lemons in half. Use a lemon juicer to juice the lemons. Then, pour the juice into the shallow dish. Be sure to remove any seeds.

9 To decorate the glasses, dip the rims into the lemon juice. Then, dip the rims in the colored sugar. Allow them to dry.

Colored sugar

10 To make the lemonade, pour the lemon juice into a pitcher. Add 6 cups of water, 4 tablespoons of sugar, and 2 teaspoons of baking soda. Stir until the sugar has dissolved and the water has turned fizzy.

11 Carefully fill each glass with lemonade.

12 Finally, put your colored ice cubes into the glasses. As the ice melts, the underwater colors will swirl through the lemonade. Serve immediately.

MUCH TASTIER THAN SALTY SEAWATER!

Cheesy Pearl Seashells

It's said that mermaids wear necklaces, bracelets, and crowns made from seashells and pearls. Serve your guest a pretty appetizer shaped like a shell with a pearl she can actually eat!

Makes 4 servings

Ingredients

- 1 teaspoon baking powder
- ¼ teaspoon salt
- 1 stick unsalted butter, cut into cubes
- ¾ cup whole wheat flour
- ¾ cup plus 1 tablespoon all-purpose flour
- ¾ cup shredded cheddar cheese
- 1 tablespoon water
- 8 ounces (226 g) cream cheese, softened
- Food coloring in the color of your choice
- 8 cocktail onions or white cheddar cheese balls

Pearl   Oyster   Shell

Pearls are precious stones that form inside the shells of oysters and clams.

Equipment

- A baking sheet
- Parchment paper
- Measuring cups and spoons
- A mixing bowl
- A wooden spoon
- A rolling pin
- A 2-inch (5-cm) round cookie cutter
- A wooden craft stick
- A small bowl
- A spoon
- A butter knife

1 Ask an adult helper to preheat the oven to 350°F (190°C) while you line the baking sheet with parchment paper.

Dough

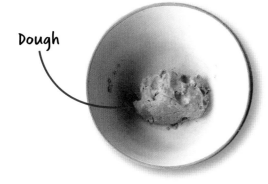

2 Measure the baking powder, salt, butter, whole wheat flour, and ¾ cups all-purpose flour into the mixing bowl. With your fingers, rub the mixture together until it looks like breadcrumbs. Then, stir in the shredded cheese with a wooden spoon.

3 Gently squeeze the mixture with your hands to form a ball of **dough**.

4 **Dust** your work surface with the tablespoon of all-purpose flour. Next, use a rolling pin to flatten the dough until it is about ½ in. (1 cm) thick.

5 Use the cookie cutter to cut as many circles as you can from the dough. Place them on the baking sheet.

6 Squeeze any remaining dough back into a ball, roll it out again, and cut as many circles as possible. Be sure to end up with an even number of circles since each seashell is made from two cheesy crackers.

7 With a craft stick, gently draw lines on half of the crackers to look like the ridges in a seashell. These crackers will be the top of each pair.

8 Ask your adult helper to put the crackers into the oven. Bake them for 15 minutes. When they are done, ask your helper to remove them from the oven and allow the cheesy shell crackers to cool completely.

> You will know the cookies are done when the edges are turning golden. Don't worry if the centers are slightly soft—they will firm up as they cool.

9 While the crackers are baking, put the cream cheese into a small bowl. Stir in two drops of food coloring. Keep adding and stirring in two drops at a time until you have the color you want.

10 When the crackers are cool, take one without ridges and use a butter knife to spread on a layer of cream cheese about ¾ in. (1.9 cm) thick. Then, take a cracker with ridges and place it on top of the cream cheese.

11 Gently push the top cracker down on one side to create the open seashell effect. Press a cocktail onion or cheese ball into the cream cheese to look like a pearl.

12 Repeat steps 10 and 11 with the remaining cheesy crackers.

YUM! *SHELL* I EAT ONE OR TWO?

Seaweed Pasta with Shrimp

There are thousands of kinds of seaweed in the ocean. Your new friend will feel right at home with this next dish full of juicy shrimp and homemade pasta that looks just like green seaweed!

Makes 4 servings

Ingredients

- 2 cups semolina flour*
- 1 teaspoon salt
- ¼ teaspoon baking powder
- 1 tablespoon butter, softened
- ½ cup warm water
- A cabbage or some kale, washed
- 2 cups of defrosted ready-cooked frozen jumbo shrimp
- Green food coloring
- ¼ cup sweet chili sauce
- ½ teaspoon black pepper

*If you can't find semolina flour, you can use whole wheat flour. It might not come together as easily, but it will still be tasty.

Equipment

- Measuring cups
- A mixing bowl
- A wooden spoon
- A dish towel
- Clean kitchen scissors
- A shallow microwave-safe dish
- A rolling pin
- A pizza cutter
- A large pot
- A large metal spoon
- An adult helper
- A timer
- A colander
- A fork and spoon

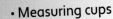

1 Put the flour, ½ teaspoon salt, and baking powder into the mixing bowl and mix with a wooden spoon.

2 Add the butter and ½ cup of warm water. Stir the mixture.

3 With your hands, squeeze the mixture into a ball and place it on your work surface. **Knead** the dough for about three minutes until it feels smooth. Put the dough back into the bowl, cover with a damp dish towel, and set aside for 30 minutes.

How do you knead dough? Repeatedly squash the dough with your palms against the work surface.

4 Use scissors to carefully cut 8 large cabbage or kale leaves lengthwise into strips that are ½ in. (1.25 cm) wide. Put to one side.

5 Lay the shrimp in a single layer in the shallow dish. Pour 1 cup of water over the shrimp so they are just covered and set aside.

6 Take the dough and gently tear it into three pieces. Dividing the dough into smaller pieces will make it easier to roll out.

7 Use the rolling pin to flatten the dough until it is about half as thick as this book's cover. Next, use the pizza cutter to cut the dough into wavy ribbons that are about ½ in. (1.25 cm) wide at their widest parts. Repeat with the other two pieces of dough.

8 Add 10 cups of water into the large pot. Add 5 drops of green food coloring and stir with a large metal spoon. Then, ask an adult helper to put the pot of water onto the stove to boil.

9 When the water has come to a boil, ask your helper to carefully drop the pasta into the water. Let the pasta cook for 2 minutes, then ask your helper to add the cabbage or kale to the water and cook for 3 more minutes.

10 While the pasta and cabbage are cooking, ask your helper to put the dish of shrimp into the microwave and heat on high for 1 minute.

11 When the pasta mixture is ready, ask your helper to drain it in a colander. Then, return it to the pot. Ask your helper to drain the hot water from the shrimp and then add the shrimp to the pot, too.

Colander —

12 Finally, add the sweet chili sauce and ½ teaspoon of salt and pepper each to the pot. Carefully **toss** the hot ingredients together with a fork and a spoon. Serve immediately.

WHO KNEW SEAWEED COULD BE SO DELICIOUS?

Magical Mermaid Ice Cream

Before your friend dives back into the ocean, it's time for dessert. What goes better with a day by the ocean than some cool, creamy ice cream? Make this perfect beachy treat with a rippling wave design.

Makes 6 servings

Ingredients

- 2 cups heavy whipping cream, chilled
- 14 oz (400 g) sweetened condensed milk, chilled
- 1 teaspoon vanilla extract
- 3 colors of food coloring your mermaid would like
- Sprinkles

Equipment

- A mixing bowl
- An electric hand mixer
- A wooden spoon
- 4 small bowls
- 3 metal spoons
- A freezer-safe plastic box, casserole dish, or cake pan that's about 3 in. (7.5 cm) deep and holds about 4 cups of liquid
- A butter knife

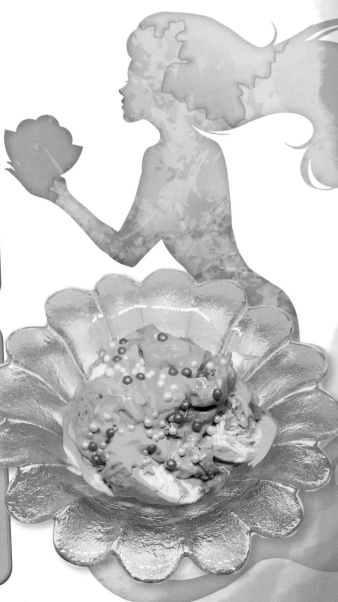

1 Pour the whipping cream into a mixing bowl. With an electric hand mixer, beat the cream until it forms soft peaks that look like little mountains.

2 Add the condensed milk and beat the mixture until it is thick and the consistency of smooth peanut butter. Stir in the vanilla extract with a wooden spoon.

Condensed milk

Vanilla extract

3 Evenly divide the mixture into four small bowls.

4 In one bowl, stir in two drops of one food coloring. Keep adding and stirring in two drops of color until you have made the color you want.

Remember to add food coloring a little at a time. You can always add more, but you can't remove it if you add too much!

5 Repeat step 4 with the second and third bowls, adding a different color to each. Leave the fourth bowl white.

6 Add a large spoonful of each color to the freezer-safe container.

7 Add some sprinkles on top of the colorful scoops.

8 Keep adding to the container one colorful spoonful at a time. This way, the colors will be mixed up and layered. Add sprinkles as you go so that they can be found between the layers.

9 When all the cream mixture is in the container, take a butter knife and gently drag it through the layers in one direction and then back in the other direction, so the colors swirl slightly.

10 Add some final sprinkles to the top and place the container in the freezer.

11 Leave the ice cream to freeze for at least 6 hours or overnight.

Frozen ice cream

A DELICIOUS END TO YOUR MEAL!

Mermaid Tales

Get to know more about your dinner guest by checking out these fascinating facts and magical **myths** about mermaids.

A mermaid is a creature with the scaly tail of a fish and the upper body of a human woman. A male half-human, half-fish creature is called a merman.

People around the world have told tall *tails* about merpeople for thousands of years. Some stories say they are evil creatures. Others tell that spotting a merperson could be good luck.

IF YOU WERE HAVING DINNER WITH A MERMAID, WHAT WOULD YOU ASK HER?

A dugong

Could mermaids be real? Probably not. Scientists think that sailors who told stories of mermaids actually spotted dugongs or manatees at sea. These animals have flat, mermaid-like tails and flippers that look similar to arms.

Glossary

appetizers small dishes of food eaten before a main meal

dough a mixture of flour, water, and other ingredients that is used to make pasta, bread, cookies, and crackers

dust to sprinkle with flour to keep dough from sticking

equipment tools or items that are used to do a job

host a person who entertains other people

ingredients the things that are used to make food

knead to squeeze dough with your hands many times

menu a list of the foods and drinks that will be served during a meal

myths old stories that tell of strange or magical events and creatures

shellfish ocean animals with a shell, such as shrimp and oysters

toss to mix a sauce or dressing into food by lifting and stirring the mixture with two spoons or other utensils

Index

cheesy pearl seashells 4, 10

dugongs 22

host 6

ice cream 4, 18

lemon ocean-ade 4, 6

manatees 22

merpeople 22

oysters 10

pearls 10, 13

safety 5, 18, 20

seaweed 4, 14, 17

seaweed pasta with shrimp 4, 14

shrimp 4, 14, 16–17

Read More

Ahrens, Niki. *Celebrate with Ariel: Plan a Little Mermaid Party (Disney Princess Celebrations)*. Minneapolis: Lerner Publications, 2020.

Williams, Samantha. *Mermaid Puzzles (Magical Puzzles)*. New York: Windmill Books, 2020.

Learn More Online

1. Go to **www.factsurfer.com**
2. Enter "**Mermaid Meals**" into the search box.
3. Click on the cover of this book to see a list of websites.

About the Author

Ruth Owen has been developing and writing children's books for more than 10 years. She lives in Cornwall, England, just minutes from the ocean. Ruth loves cooking and making up recipes. Her favorite dish in this book is the mermaid ice cream.